GEORGE

Gets Dressed

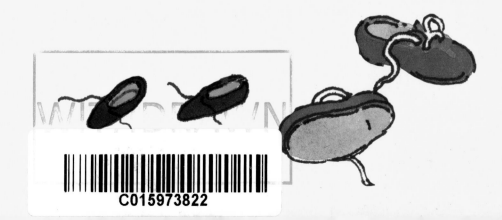

GEO

Nicola Smee

RGE
Gets Dressed

ORCHARD

My bear's bare and
so am I.

I think we'd better
get dressed.

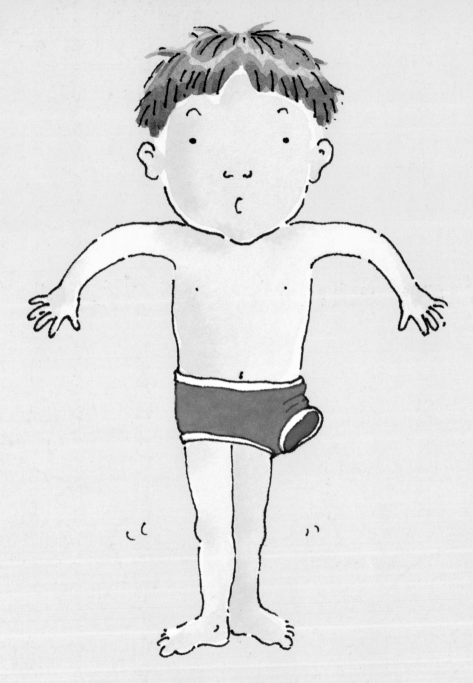

Pants for me

and pants for Bear.

T-shirt for me and
t-shirt for Bear.

Socks for me

and socks for Bear.

Trousers for me and . . .

I think a skirt for
Bear today.

Shoes for me and
shoes for Bear.

Yoo-hoo!
Bath time,
George!

Oh no! It's back to being bare, Bear!

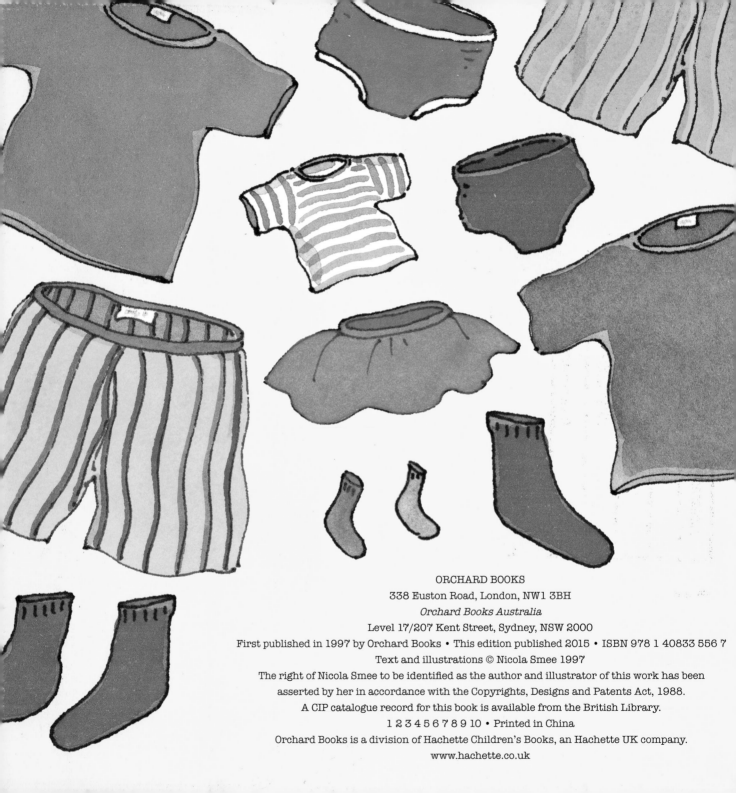

ORCHARD BOOKS
338 Euston Road, London, NW1 3BH
Orchard Books Australia
Level 17/207 Kent Street, Sydney, NSW 2000
First published in 1997 by Orchard Books • This edition published 2015 • ISBN 978 1 40833 556 7
Text and illustrations © Nicola Smee 1997
The right of Nicola Smee to be identified as the author and illustrator of this work has been
asserted by her in accordance with the Copyrights, Designs and Patents Act, 1988.
A CIP catalogue record for this book is available from the British Library.
1 2 3 4 5 6 7 8 9 10 • Printed in China
Orchard Books is a division of Hachette Children's Books, an Hachette UK company.
www.hachette.co.uk